Franklin and Harriet

For Shane and Keeley, brother and sister — P.B.
To Derek, who knows all about baby sisters — B.C.

Franklin is a trademark of Kids Can Press Ltd.

Text © 2001 Context*x* Inc.
Illustrations © 2001 Brenda Clark Illustrator Inc.

Interior illustrations prepared with the assistance of Shelley Southern.

Kids Can Press acknowledges the financial support of the Ontario
Arts Council, the Canada Council for the Arts and the Government
of Canada, through the BPIDP, for our publishing activity.

Published in Canada by
Kids Can Press Ltd.
25 Dockside Drive
Toronto, ON M5A 0B5

www.kidscanpress.com

Edited by Tara Walker

The hardcover edition of this book is smyth sewn casebound.
The paperback edition of this book is limp sewn with a drawn-on cover.
Manufactured in Buji, Shenzhen, China, in 10/2010 by WKT Company

CM 01 0 9 8 7 6 5 4 3 2
CDN PA 01 0 9 8 7 6 5 4 3

Library and Archives Canada Cataloguing in Publication

Bourgeois, Paulette
        Franklin and Harriet / written by Paulette Bourgeois ; illustrated
by Brenda Clark.

ISBN 978-1-55453-727-3

1. Franklin (Fictitious character : Bourgeois) — Juvenile fiction. I. Clark,
Brenda II. Title.

PS8553.O85477F856 2011   jC813'.54   C2010-906673-1

Kids Can Press is a *l'orus*™ Entertainment company

Franklin and Harriet

Written by Paulette Bourgeois
Illustrated by Brenda Clark

Kids Can Press

FRANKLIN could count by twos and tie his shoes.
He helped his little sister, Harriet, zip zippers and
button buttons. He showed her how to play peekaboo
and pat-a-cake. He read stories and sang songs to her.
Franklin loved his little sister, and he liked being a
big brother ... most of the time.

One day, Franklin took Harriet outside to play.
He pushed Harriet in her swing.
He held her hand as she went down the slide.
But he didn't see the puddle at the bottom.

"Oh, no!" cried Franklin.

Harriet was covered in mud.

Franklin looked around. Maybe he could clean her up before his father noticed.

Harriet rubbed her face, and it got muddy, too. Then she started to cry.

"Please don't cry," begged Franklin.

He gave Harriet her blanket. He made funny faces. But nothing stopped her sobbing.

Then Franklin had an idea. He pretended that his stuffed dog, Sam, was a puppet.

Franklin barked. Harriet smiled.

"Bad mud puddle!" said Franklin.

Harriet giggled. She reached out to Sam and gave him a hug.

"Whew!" said Franklin.

Franklin's father laughed when he saw Harriet. "I think a bubble bath is in order."

Franklin was relieved. "Sam needs one, too."

"Two baths coming up," said Franklin's father.

Franklin helped fill the tub and stir up the bubbles. He checked to make sure the water was not too hot and not too cold.

Just before bedtime, Franklin couldn't find
Sam anywhere.

Finally, he spotted Sam in Harriet's crib.

Franklin wanted Sam back, but his mother didn't
want to wake Harriet.

"Perhaps Harriet could sleep with Sam just this
once," she suggested.

Franklin didn't like that one bit. But he didn't
want Harriet to cry again either.

"All right," he sighed. "Only for tonight."

The next morning, Harriet brought Sam to breakfast.
"Thanks, Harriet," said Franklin, reaching for his dog.
But Harriet clung tightly to Sam.
Franklin tugged on Sam's tail. Harriet tugged back.

"He's mine!" said Franklin.

"No, mine!" shouted Harriet.

They pushed and pulled until something terrible happened.

Sam's tail ripped right off.
Franklin and Harriet started to cry.
"Oh, dear," said their mother.
"Can you fix him?" asked Franklin.
"I'll try," she answered.
Franklin gave Harriet a nasty look.

Franklin's mother used small, careful stitches to put Sam back together again.

"Good as new!" she said.

Franklin put a bandage on Sam's tail and gave him a big hug.

Harriet tried to hug Sam, too, but Franklin held Sam up high so she couldn't reach him.

"It would be nice if you shared Sam," said Franklin's mother.

Franklin didn't think it would be nice at all. He held Sam tightly and stomped off to his room.

Franklin decided that being a big brother could be a big problem.

Harriet cried a lot. She needed to be watched every minute. Sometimes she was stinky.

And worst of all, she thought that Sam was hers.

So Franklin did what any big brother would do. He put Sam in the toy box at the back of the cupboard, where Harriet couldn't find him.

Later, Franklin's mother asked if he wanted to go for a walk.

"Is Harriet coming?" asked Franklin.

His mother nodded.

Franklin sighed. But he got ready to go because he liked walks.

Harriet put on her coat upside down and backwards.

"That looks silly," sniffed Franklin.

His mother laughed and helped Harriet with her coat.

On their walk, Franklin picked a bouquet of dandelions for his mother.

"Thank you," she said. "They're lovely."

Just then, Harriet grabbed the flowers.

"No, Harriet," said Franklin. "Those aren't yours."

Franklin's mother smiled. "Harriet is still little," she said. "She needs to learn how to share."

Franklin's mother took some of the flowers and tucked them into her hat.

Harriet put her flowers into her mouth.

Franklin hoped they tasted terrible.

They walked for a long time.

Harriet began to rub her eyes and yawn. Then she got cranky.

Franklin's mother gave Harriet her blanket, a cookie and some juice.

But nothing made Harriet happy. She started to cry. She got louder and louder.

"Too bad Sam's not here," said Franklin. "He could make her stop crying."

Then Franklin had an idea. He put Harriet's blanket over his hand and barked.

Harriet giggled.

"It's not Sam who makes Harriet happy," said Franklin's mother. "It's her big brother."

"Really?" said Franklin.

"Really," she answered.

Franklin walked a little taller.

Franklin decided that being a big brother was a good thing after all.

He liked to make Harriet laugh.

Sometimes, he even let her play with Sam.

But Franklin always made sure that Sam was back in his room by bedtime.

There is only so much sharing a big brother can do.